TOMORROW
POWER

Hazy BLOOM
AND THE TOMORROW POWER

pictures by
Jennifer Hamburg   Jenn Harney

SQUARE FISH

FARRAR STRAUS GIROUX · NEW YORK

SQUARE
FISH

An imprint of Macmillan Publishing Group, LLC
175 Fifth Avenue
New York, NY 10010
mackids.com

Our books may be purchased in bulk for promotional, educational, or business use. Please contact your local bookseller or the Macmillan Corporate
and Premium Sales Department at (800) 221-7945 ext. 5442 or by e-mail
at MacmillanSpecialMarkets@macmillan.com.

Library of Congress Cataloging-in-Publication Data`

Names: Hamburg, Jennifer, author. | Harney, Jennifer, illustrator.
Title: Hazy Bloom and the tomorrow power / Jennifer Hamburg ;
    pictures by Jenn Harney.
Description: New York : Farrar Straus Giroux, 2017. |
    Series: Hazy Bloom | Summary: When third-grader Hazel "Hazy"
    Bloom begins having visions of trouble that will come within twenty-
    four hours, she finds that this mysterious power provides her the
    ability to make things worse.
Identifiers: LCCN 2016024328 (print) | LCCN 2016052852 (ebook) |
    ISBN 978-1-250-14355-6 (paperback)   ISBN 978-0-374-30496-6 (ebook)
Subjects: | CYAC: Extrasensory perception—Fiction. | Family life—
    Fiction. | Schools—Fiction. | Humorous stories. | BISAC: JUVENILE
    FICTION / Humorous Stories. | JUVENILE FICTION / Mysteries &
    Detective Stories.
Classification: LCC PZ7.H1756 Haz 2017 (print) | LCC PZ7.H1756 (ebook) |
    DDC [Fic]—dc23
LC record available at https://lccn.loc.gov/2016024328

Originally published in the United States by Farrar Straus Giroux
First Square Fish Edition: 2018
Book designed by Elizabeth H. Clark
Square Fish logo designed by Filomena Tuosto

1   3   5   7   9   10   8   6   4   2

AR: 4.8/LEXILE: 730L

To J for the chapter-one chat.

To M for the word woohooing.

And to my original Hazy. Keep being hilarious.

—Jen

To Colleen

—Jenn

Hazy Bloom AND THE TOMORROW POWER

The first vision I ever had came on Sunday, and I know this because I was staring at the fridge.

Well, not just the plain old fridge, because that would be weird.

I was staring at the school cafeteria menu *on* the fridge. Mom puts the weekly lunch menu on the fridge every Sunday, in the very same spot each time: between our family calendar and the "reminder" board where we are supposed to write reminder-y things like *Get milk* or *Remember library book*, but where my brother usually draws cartoons of insects burping or monsters sitting on the toilet. The point is, my brother's annoying. And

also, that it was defi-
nitely Sunday.

I put my finger up to
Monday on the menu
and slid it down to the
right spot. Then I squealed.
"Pizza dippers!"

If you don't know what pizza dippers are,
you've got a lot of living to do. But I'll go ahead
and tell you that pizza dippers are long sticks of
bread with gooey cheese inside and you dip the
whole thing in pizza sauce. They are extremely
delicious. Which is why I then said, "Yay-yay-
yay-yay-yay-yay-yay!"

"Ay!" chirped The Baby, who was sitting on
the floor trying to eat Cheerios with a fork. The
Baby has an actual name, which is Alexander,
but everyone else calls him "The Baby," so I do,
too. And he doesn't even seem to mind, which is
odd because I wouldn't want everyone calling

me "The Girl" or "The Middle One." But I guess he's okay with that kind of thing.

Mom peered over my shoulder at the menu. "Ooh, pizza dippers. Lucky you. And lucky me—one less lunch to make," she said with a wink.

"Yup, 'cause I'm having"—I took a deep breath, opened up my arms, and sang at the top of my lungs—"piiiiiiiiiiiiiiiiiizza dip—"

I stopped singing. Because suddenly my arms started to get prickly and goose bumpy, and I kind of felt hot and cold at the same time. And then—well, remember that vision I mentioned? That's when it happened, right there, in front of the fridge, my mom, and The Baby, who was now using his fork to hurl Cheerios at our dog, Mr. Cheese. It was like a picture only I could see. But it wasn't a normal picture, like of my family, or me on my birthday.

This is what it was a picture of:

Flying peas

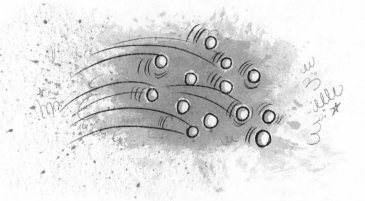

That's right. Little, round, green peas, flying around in midair. And then, the picture was gone.

Very. Strange. Especially because I'm not even that fond of peas.

"You okay, Hazy?" Mom asked. I guess I was still staring at the fridge.

"Um, yeah, I just . . . saw something," I said. Mom gave me a funny look and opened her mouth like she was going to ask more. Then everything went bananas. The Baby spit up some mushed

Cheerios just as my brother Milo ran into the house from soccer practice, followed by my dad, who immediately tripped over Mr. Cheese. (My dad always trips over Mr. Cheese. I don't know if he doesn't see Mr. Cheese, or if Mr. Cheese tries to trip him on purpose, but the point is, if you're ever at my house, just please look down when you walk in the kitchen door. There might be a dog.)

"Hazel, don't just stand there. Please do something!" Mom pleaded.

I guess I wasn't being very helpful. I grabbed The Baby so I didn't have to clean up his disgusting regurgitation, and by the time I changed him, my dad got his throw-uppy clothes into the washing

machine, and my brother got sent to his room for saying "Gross!" again and again and again, I didn't really get a chance to talk to anyone about the flying peas. But that was fine with me. I didn't want to think about them anyway. It weirded me out, for real live. Instead, I decided to turn to more important things.

I headed to my room to work on my space mission to Mars.

2

My plan to become an astronaut started with our "Curious Kids" science project at school. We had to pick something we were curious about and do a report on it. Some kids were curious about thunderstorms, others were curious about sharks. I was curious about how many mini-marshmallows would fit up my nose. (I bet you thought I was going to say, "Space travel"! Don't worry, it's coming. Keep reading.)

When I explained my nose-marshmallow idea to my teacher, Mrs. Agnes, she asked me if I could come up with a more "educational" idea, and then I asked *her* if there were rules for being curious about mini-marshmallows and she told me no, but it *was* a rule to behave safely, and sticking marshmallows of any size up one's nose did not appear to be a safe classroom activity.

Of course, I decided to prove her wrong. The next day, I brought a bagful of mini-marshmallows to school and started stuffing them up there in my nostrils in front of a small circle of my friends during Silent Reading. As soon as Mrs. Agnes caught sight of what I was doing, she marched me straight to the nurse's office. The nurse, who was as alarmed as Mrs. Agnes, made me take them all out, and then had me sit there and rest for *twenty whole minutes* just in case I had permanently damaged myself in some way, which I totally had not. The point is, the answer to my mini-marshmallow question was six per nostril. And also, as I was sitting there bored out of my mind, the nurse handed me a book to pass the time, and that book was about Mars.

Before long, I had learned all of these amazing things, like it's a mystery whether there is any water at all on Mars and even if there is, the average surface temperature is minus fifty-eight degrees. I also learned the following: *no human has ever been to Mars.*

And that got me thinking: if I get there first, I can make the rules! And the first rule would be that if you want to stick mini-marshmallows up your nose, that's your business. Also, I'd offer ice-skating lessons. Might as well make use of the cold weather.

Since that day, I've been carefully planning my space mission, and if I say so myself, it is going pretty well!

I pulled my Mars Space Mission notebook from my bookshelf and  flipped it open to the page called "Finance," which is all the stuff about money. I figured I would need about seven million dollars to rent a rocket ship to get me to Mars (which is at least thirty-four million miles away, did you know that?), and after digging through my pockets from yesterday, I now had . . . eight dollars and fifty-three cents. So I was on track.

Now it was time for the next order of business: my space outfits. I started rummaging through my clothes (in addition to being freezing cold, Mars sometimes also gets really hot,

so I concluded that the answer was layering). Soon, though, my thoughts returned to the flying peas.

What *was* that weird vision thing that happened in the kitchen? Had I been remembering something? I figured I would remember flying peas if I had seen them before. Maybe it was something I had dreamed about? But I didn't recall any dreams about peas, or any vegetable, for that matter. Especially ones flying through the air.

I shook my head hard, willing my thoughts away. *Forget it*, I instructed myself. *It was probably a daydream. A really weird, totally random daydream about flying peas. It could happen.*

Once I told myself that, I didn't think about the peas at all, like ever again.

Until lunchtime the next day.

3

Rrrrrrrrrrring! The Monday lunch bell snapped me out of my spelling-test stupor. Third grade seemed to be all about spelling, and I would like to know why I'll ever need to know how to spell *wrinkle*, or *quotient*, or *camPAIGN*, which I believe is a word you would use to describe my older brother. Personally, I think it is much more important to learn to spell words like *disgusting* and *regurgitation*, which are much more useful, especially when The Baby is around. The point is, it was now time to eat.

"Come on, Hazy Bloom. Let's get in line. The first dippers are the freshest." Elizabeth grabbed my hand and steered me toward the cafeteria.

Elizabeth Almeida is my BFSB, which stands for "best friend since birth," because, that's right, we met right after we were born—well, not like that *minute* because we were busy crying and dealing with the issue of being birthed and stuff—but very soon after, when both our moms took a Mommy and Me yoga class together at the Y (we were the "me's"). During the class, our moms found out they lived one street away from each other. They became great friends, and Elizabeth and I did, too. Of course, Elizabeth and I don't remember meeting back then or going to the yoga class at all, but we're pretty sure it's the reason we can both do excellent backbends.

Besides yoga, Elizabeth and I have a lot in

common. We both hate puppets. We both have a *z* in our name. We both wish we had braces. And we both love pizza dippers. Also, Elizabeth is the only person who *always* calls me Hazy Bloom, which is my preferred version of my name. So there's that.

Elizabeth and I got our dippers and walked over to our table. Well, it's not our table like we own it, but we sit there every day so it's kind of the same. The twins, Lila and Derrick, were already there. As usual, they were wearing sports-team jerseys. Lila's was really bright orange, and Derrick's was really bright green, so to-

gether they really made my eyes hurt. It is just my opinion, but I believe that as twins, they have a responsibility to color coordinate, at least if they're going to sit side by side. Anyway, they were chatting about the Spring Spectacular, the big school carnival coming up next week.

"I've been practicing my face-painting designs," Lila was saying. "So far I can draw a butterfly, a rose, and a shooting star."

"What about a mouse?" Derrick asked.

Lila looked at her brother. "Who'd want a mouse painted on their face?"

"Someone who likes animals, like me. That's

why I signed up for the petting zoo. There's going to be sheep, miniature goats, ducks, I think a pig, some chickens . . ."

The Spring Spectacular was the most fun event of the whole school year, mainly because the students were in charge, which is how school should be all the time. The fifth graders picked the theme (this year it was "Flower Power," for spring), the fourth graders chose the games and rides, and the third graders (that's us, in case you forgot) would each get to volunteer at a carnival station. We could choose from: face painting (Lila), games (Anthony, Deacon, and May), petting zoo (Derrick and Zoe), raffle (Shelby), tickets (Joanna), bake sale (Elizabeth and me!), dunk tank (Caleb), or cleanup crew (no one). Because nobody chose cleanup crew, Mrs. Agnes said she'd have to choose somebody "at a later date," which we all knew meant if someone got in trouble between now and the day of the carnival, that person would end up being on the cleanup crew.

"Oh, and a baby llama!" Derrick was still going on about the petting zoo.

"Can we please stop talking about farm animals while we're eating?" Lila said. "My sandwich is starting to smell like *manure*" (not a spelling word, but totally should be because it is hilarious, for real live).

"Let's talk about the bake sale," Elizabeth suggested. "This year there's going to be a cupcake contest, and guess what? The winners get a free week at Camp Showbiz! Seriously, *a free week at theater camp!*"

So the thing is, Elizabeth likes to perform. A lot. She's constantly making up skits and casting herself in the lead, and then I end up playing the lamp or the pumpkin or the howling wind (which, let me tell you, is not as easy as it sounds). I'd like to ask Elizabeth why I can't ever be just a plain old person and not some dumb thing in the background, but I know why. It's because Elizabeth is always the star. I've learned not to argue with that.

Anyway, it would be a dream come true for her to win the free week at theater camp, especially because her mom told her the camp was too expensive and she couldn't go otherwise. I'd personally rather go to space camp, but since my best friend really wanted this, I was all in. Also, I'm not aware of any space camps in Denver that prepare you for Mars. The point is, we had big plans to win the contest.

"Hazy Bloom and I are going to make a ginormous cupcake tower," Elizabeth was explaining.

"Gi-normous," I repeated just to get the point across.

"What's a cupcake tower?" asked Lila.

"You don't *know*?" I said. Then I stopped because I had no idea either.

Elizabeth took over, using animated hand movements to demonstrate. "Okay, a cupcake tower is when you have a bunch of round trays with little stands underneath, and then you stack the trays on top of each other. Then you put cupcakes all around each one."

She gestured triumphantly to her imaginary creation. "Ta-da! A cupcake tower." She ended with a bow. (See? Born for the stage!)

Derrick said, "Cool! How many trays will there be?"

I jumped in. "*A lot*. Like fifty."

"Well, like six," Elizabeth said.

"Exactly," I said.

Do you see how well we work together? It's no wonder we're best friends. We were totally going to win that free week at theater camp. Maybe we'll do a play about astronauts.

"Hey," I said. "We should decorate the cupcakes with little flowers for spring."

"That's what *I* was thinking!" Elizabeth exclaimed. I could tell she felt good about our plan. I leaned over to take a cheesy, pizza-dipper-y bite, and that's when I saw something annoying at the other end of the table. That something was Luke.

Luke has been in my class since kindergarten and my nickname for him is Mapefrl, which I know is not easy to say but cannot be changed because it stands for "most annoying person ever, for real live." I don't know if he tries to be annoying or if being annoying simply comes naturally, but the point is, he must be taking lessons from my brother. Those two have a lot in common.

Anyway, I normally wouldn't be paying attention to Mapefrl, but at that moment, out of the corner of my eye, I saw him grab some food off his lunch tray and throw it at me. I couldn't tell what it was, but something about it seemed oddly familiar. Anyway, whatever he threw missed me completely, but his total rudeness made Elizabeth mad, so she stood up and flung a pizza dipper right back at him. Unfortunately, it didn't get Mapefrl, but it smushed right into Shelby's shoulder.

Between you and me, pizza dippers smushed all over someone's shoulder suddenly don't look very tasty. Anyway, Shelby grabbed some crackers and threw those across the table. Then Lila threw her jelly sandwich. Derrick threw string cheese. All of a sudden, there were cookies, chocolate milk, pickles, and yogurt being flung

all over the cafeteria, including a bagel that would have gotten me in the forehead, but I dodged it just in time. It was a full-on food fight. I watched as Mapefrl gleefully lobbed handfuls of food, cackling away. And that's when I noticed what he was throwing, what he'd been throwing all along, and specifically, what had started the entire food fight.

It was peas. *Flying peas.*

I thought about yesterday and the prickles and goose bumps and the weird vision thingy I saw in front of the fridge. All of a sudden, I realized what it was I had seen. I saw this crazy food fight.

The day before it happened.

4

Mapefrl was put on the cleanup crew for the carnival. Mrs. Agnes said it was a consequence of starting the food fight. The rest of us had a consequence, too, which was to do extra spelling homework, which now included the word *consequence*. I probably would have been more annoyed about the homework, except I was currently freaking out about the flying peas. It was practically *impossible* (spelling word) to *concentrate* (spelling word) on anything else for the rest of the day, so when the dismissal bell finally rang, I sprinted over to Elizabeth in about one second flat.

"Okay, for real live, can I tell you something one thousand percent weird?" I said.

Elizabeth looked at me. "Is it about hairballs or potato salad?"

"It is not," I promised.

In case you ever need to have a conversation with Elizabeth, you should know that hairballs and potato salad are the two things she does not like to talk about, ever. I don't know why it's those two particular things but the point is, I like potato salad so don't worry about bringing it up to me. Also, *hairballs* should totally be a spelling word. It comes up a lot more than *campaign*.

I told Elizabeth about the flying peas, how I saw them in my head yesterday in the kitchen, and then today how I saw the *same thing* for real live in the cafeteria, and how it was all just totally bananas, which come to think of it, were pretty much the only food that wasn't involved in the whole *ordeal* (spelling word).

After I was done talking, Elizabeth looked at me like I had a tree growing out of my ear. "Okay, Hazy Bloom. Let me get this straight. Yesterday in your head you saw a bunch of peas flying through the air—"

"Yes."

"And today there was a food fight."

"Yes."

"With flying peas."

"Among other things."

"Which means you saw the food fight happen before it happened?"

"Yes."

I could tell Elizabeth was letting everything roll around in her brain. Then she said, "So . . . wait. Does that mean . . . ?"

"Does that mean what?"

A slow,

giddy smile spread across her face. "Does that mean you saw the future?" She continued. "Yes, it does! You *saw* the future!"

In case you were keeping track, Elizabeth just asked and answered her own question. She does this sometimes when she gets excited. I guess it's easier than talking to another whole person.

"Okay, hold the phone there, girlie," I said. "It's an expression," I explained when she looked around for a phone. "I *cannot* see the future."

"But you already *did* see the future, didn't you? Yes, you did!"

See what I mean about answering her own question?

Then she goes, "It's like you have a super-power!"

This was too much. "Look, it was one vision. About the future. That happened to come true. It might not ever happen again."

"Or it might *will* happen again!" Elizabeth practically howled.

I stared at my best friend. "That's a crazy sentence that doesn't make any sense."

"I mean that it could easily happen again," she said quickly. Then she turned toward me and got really close, like she was about to say the most serious thing in the world. Or spit on me. I couldn't quite tell but I hoped it was the first one. "Listen to me, Hazy Bloom. You need to have another vision to figure out if this whole seeing-the-future thing is real."

I threw my arms up in the air. "How? How am I supposed to do that? Wave my magic wand? Use my cauldron?"

"Don't be ridiculous, cauldrons are for witches. Anyway, I don't know how, you just need to try! And if it happens again, you'll call me immediately, right? Yes, of course you will."

Elizabeth finished the conversation with herself, then waved goodbye and skipped down the street to her house.

I did a halfhearted wave back. My head was spinning at the strangeness of it all. Could I really see the future? Did I truly have some kind of superpower?

I guess if it happened again, I'd know the answer.

5

"Hazel Hillary Bloom, what on earth are you doing?"

It was dinnertime that same day, and my mom was talking to me like I was nuts. And maybe I did look a little strange. My nose was pressed right up against the fridge. I had been standing that way for fifteen minutes.

"Checking the lunch menu."

"You're a little . . . close, no?"

Okay, I wasn't checking the lunch menu, because if I had been I would have seen that it said *Bean burrito* and then I would have said, *Gross*, and walked away. I was trying to have another vision. It wasn't working.

"Move back, you're going to give yourself a headache," Mom said. She plopped The Baby down in his high chair and gave him some animal crackers. "Have you done your homework?"

"Yes, please."

"Hazel, are you listening?"

Fine, I wasn't listening.

Then Milo came in. "Excuse me!" he said, which you might think sounded polite but was not because he had flung open the fridge with me standing in front of it, knocking me backward.

"Hey! Hey, hey, hey, hey, hey!" I yelled at him.

He ignored me and grabbed the peanut butter.

Mom turned a laser glare my way. "Seri-

ously, Hazel, why are you acting this way?"
Then she zapped my brother. "Milo, no snack-
ing. We're eating dinner soon. Please go tell
your dad I need his help."

"*Daaaaaaaad!*" Milo shrieked.

I don't think that's what my mom meant.

I saw that The Baby was licking the back of
every animal cracker on his tray. Not eating,
just licking. He was so *bizarre* (spelling word,
and a perfect description of my entire family).

I took a deep breath. "Mom, it's just there's something important I want to practice—I mean, see—I mean, do," I said.

"What's soooooo important?" asked Milo, who was still trying to sneak-eat a spoonful of peanut butter that did not make it into his mouth, because at that moment my dad walked in and without even stopping took the spoon from Milo and put it in the sink.

"Nice try, kid," Dad said.

Pretty smooth move by Dad, I had to admit. Then he tripped over the dog again.

I turned to Milo. "If you must know, I have discovered a new power and I'd like to work on it."

"Is it annoying power?" he said, cracking himself up.

Did I mention that Milo is not hilarious?

I put my hands on my hips. "No. That's your specialty."

41

Ha! I looked at my mom, thinking she'd high-five me and say, "Good one, Hazy Bloom!" but all I got was, "Hazel. Homework. Now." She didn't even call me by my preferred name.

"Rrrrrrrrrrrmph!" I replied.

"Ha!" said the annoying one.

"Ga!" said The Baby.

We all looked at him. He had stuck the licked animal crackers all over his entire face. He looked like a cheetah with animal-shaped spots.

"Oh, for goodness' sake," Mom said, and started plucking the goopy animal crackers off. Without even looking at me she said in a warning tone, "Hazel . . . go."

"Fine!" I said in my huffiest voice possible. "But just so you know, I might be able to see the future!"

Nobody responded. Dad was taking over dinner duty, Mom was whisking The Baby away for a quick bath, and Milo had headed off to work on his ghost costume for the haunted house (the Spring Spectacular Haunted House was another thing the fifth graders were in charge of, and Milo was in fifth grade, even though he usually acts like he is in kindergarten, for real live).

I trudged down the hall to my room.

On the way, I stopped and stared hard at the wall and counted silently: *One . . . two . . . three . . . four.* No vision.

Later, when I was doing the homework I had silently refused to start until after dinner as a protest against my family's unfairness, I stared at a sentence on my Language Arts handout until the letters all melted together. Nothing.

In the bath, I stared at the bubbles until my eyes crossed. All I saw was bubbles.

After I put on my PJs and gave my fish their dinner, I stared inside the fish tank. My fish stared back at me. It was incredibly boring. And I didn't see a vision anyway.

Two more days went by, and still, no visions. By Wednesday night, I had pretty much given up. The flying peas must have been a onetime thing. Or maybe I even imagined it altogether. Whatever it was, one thing seemed clear: I could not see the future.

Then, that night, as I was brushing my teeth, my arms suddenly got all prickly and goose bumpy, and I felt hot and cold at the same time.

I peered into the sink and right next to the toothpaste I had just spit out, a big, blue, sparkly number stared back at me.

6

"Tell me! Tell me everything! What did you see?"

It was recess the next day, and Elizabeth and I were sitting under the oak tree at the edge of the playground. Elizabeth didn't ride the bus that morning, and this was our first chance to talk about my vision from last night.

A bumblebee was buzzing around us, which normally

might have freaked me out, but today I barely noticed because I was so excited to tell her what I saw.

"Okay," I said to my friend. "Shoo!" I said to the bee, who seemed to hear me and buzzed away. I turned my attention back to Elizabeth. I smiled broadly. "I saw a number."

Elizabeth looked perplexed. "A what?"

"A number," I repeated.

"That's it?" she said.

"Yes, that's it!" I said, a little insulted that my vision of the future wasn't interesting enough for her.

Elizabeth pondered this. "Where did you see it?" she asked.

"In the bathroom sink."

"Weird."

"I know!"

We took a moment to observe Lila and Derrick passing a soccer ball back and forth across the grass. They were wearing team jerseys again, but this time the colors looked much better together—Derrick's was red and Lila's was blue with shiny dots. For once, they weren't clashing. Then I heard Elizabeth say, "What number?"

"What?" I turned back to her.

"What number did you see? *In your vision*," she whispered, even though no one was around.

"Fourteen," I said confidently. Then I paused. "Or forty-one. Or maybe nine."

Elizabeth threw her arms up, *exasperated* (spelling word). "Hazy Bloom, your entire vision was a number and you don't even remember the number?"

"It was nine. Definitely nine. Probably, definitely nine," I said.

Elizabeth rolled her eyes. "And what does the number even *mean*?"

I thought about it for a minute. "Maybe . . . it's the number to a secret door somewhere in

our school! And
maybe . . . behind
that door is some-
thing terri-
fying, like
a family of
giant rats

with sharp, deadly fangs! Or maybe it's a big
hunk of moldy cheese! *Or* . . . a rat family *with*
moldy cheese and they're planning to *use* the
cheese to stink up the whole school!"

Elizabeth stared at me. "Or," she said calmly,
"maybe it's a number we need to know for our
math quiz . . . ?"

"That's ridiculous," I replied.

"Oh, *that's* ridiculous?" Elizabeth snapped.
"But a family of giant rats attacking the school
with moldy cheese is a perfectly good explana-
tion?"

I groaned. We weren't getting anywhere.

What was the use of seeing a vision of the future if I couldn't figure out what that vision meant? I got up and headed to the water fountain. All this thinking was making me thirsty.

On the field, Derrick and Lila were now both running toward the soccer ball, which sat midway between them. Lila got to it first and kicked it hard across the grass. It rolled toward me and landed at my feet. As Lila ran over to get it, I bent down to pick it up so I could give it back to her. I straightened up with the ball in my hands, and that's when I got a good look at the front of her shirt.

It had a big, blue, sparkly number nine on it.

My vision was about Lila! But what *about*

her? Was there something important about Lila's shirt? Something else I needed to see? To do? I looked around for something, anything that could give me more information. I was at a loss.

The bumblebee was back, swirling around me, interrupting my train of thought. What did it want from me, anyway? I shooed it away again.

Lila stopped in front of me to get the ball. And that's when I remembered last year, when Lila got stung on the face by a bee, and her lip swelled up so badly she had to go to the hospital.

I looked around anxiously for the bee, which, of course, was now nowhere to be found. Where had it gone? It seemed to have vanished. Then, it occurred to me to look at the soccer ball, still in my hands. I rotated it halfway around. The bee was there.

Lila raised her hands to grab the ball from me.

"*Stop!*" I screamed, dropping the ball and kicking it and the stinging insect away.

"Hey! What'd you do that for?" Lila said.

"Bee," was all I could manage to say.

Lila's eyes grew wide. "Oh, wow! I didn't see it. That was a close one. You know I'm totally allergic, right?"

I nodded, too dazed to speak.

"Thanks, Hazy!
Thank you so much!"
She gave me a grateful hug,
then raced back to Derrick, who
had retrieved the ball. I saw her
gesturing wildly and pointing at me with a
big, relieved smile.

Elizabeth ran up to me, wanting to know every detail. "Wow!" she said after I told her. "So your vision kept Lila from getting stung by a bee? You, like, practically saved her life!" Then she leaned close and whispered, "You totally have a superpower."

I started to smile. I was beginning to think she was right.

7

That night, I was in my room talking to Elizabeth on the phone. We were working on our cupcake contest plan, which began with me asking why we needed a cupcake contest plan. I mean, making cupcakes seemed fairly straightforward, as you just . . . made the cupcakes, right?

Clearly I had never made cupcakes with Elizabeth.

"Here's how it's going to work," Elizabeth began. "Today is Thursday. So on Friday, Saturday, and Sunday, we'll experiment with different cupcake recipes and find the *absolute best* one. Remember, no boxed stuff! Only made-from-scratch recipes for the batter and frosting, understand? Yes, you understand."

There she went, having a conversation with herself again.

She continued, "Okay, so then on Monday we'll set up our baking station and ingredients, on Tuesday and Wednesday we'll bake and decorate, and then on Thursday morning we'll bring the finished cupcakes to school, which leaves plenty of time before the Spring Spectacular two days later, on Saturday. Do you agree with this plan?"

I wondered what would happen if I did not. I was too scared to find out.

"I agree," I said.

"Okay, next order of business!" Elizabeth announced like the president of the world.

Happily, the next order of business was discussing my new superpower. Elizabeth's idea was for me to use my power to get pizza dippers on the menu for the rest of the year. My idea was to find out when Mapefrl was going to the bathroom and then make sure there was no toilet paper.

We were cracking up about this when I heard a knock on the door. My mom came in. "Hazel, I need to talk to you for a sec."

I put my hand over the phone and looked at her. "Excuse me, I'm on the phone," I said politely but firmly.

Mom put her hand on her hip and did her laser glare at me.

"I'll call you back," I muttered to Elizabeth, and hung up.

Mom said, "You need to start cleaning your room."

"For what?" I said, looking around. I thought my room actually looked neater than usual.

"For Aunt Jenna," Mom replied.

I snapped my head back to Mom. "Aunt Jenna's coming?" I said in a surprised and maybe not-so-nice voice.

Mom sighed her pretend sigh that I know isn't real because it is so loud there's no way anyone would sigh that way unless they were just doing it to be dramatic. Trust me, I've heard Elizabeth do it a million times.

"Yes, Aunt Jenna's coming," she said.

So here's the thing: my aunt Jenna is very nice but also kind of, well, odd. For example, she always brings me presents but they're kooky presents, like a thumb piano from Mozambique, or a talking pen from Japan. And yes, sometimes they end up being sort of cool, and even useful, like the time Elizabeth wanted to show me what "interpretive dance" meant and needed music and I had the thumb piano right in my backpack. The point is, I would like to visit Mozambique someday. I've heard you can ride bikes everywhere, which sounds like a delightful way to travel. It certainly beats the school bus. And also, I forgot Aunt Jenna was coming.

"I told you last week," Mom was saying impatiently. "Aunt Jenna's coming tomorrow and she's sleeping in your room—"

"She's sleeping in my room?"

Mom pretend-sighed again.

"Where am *I* going to sleep?"

"With Milo."

"With Milo?" I not-so-pretend-gagged like

I was choking on a chicken leg. "But—but his room stinks!"

Milo popped his head in. "I'll make sure your side of the bed is extra-stinky," he said, and walked away.

"Rrrrrrrrrrrmph!" I replied.

Mom calmly said it was just for the week, and it was going to be great fun to have her sister here. Then she reminded me that Aunt Jenna doesn't get to visit that often because she lives far away in Maryland, and we needed to make her feel welcome. I did not agree. How was

I going to work on my superpower if I had to spend time with my weird aunt and share a room with my annoying brother?

Mom told me I should start by moving some of my clothes into Milo's room, and then I could get to the cleaning part. Then she left. Clearly, I had to do what she said. But it didn't mean I would do it quietly.

I stomped over to my closet and started yanking a bunch of clothes down from the hangers, storming into Milo's room, and dumping the clothes on his floor. Back and forth, yank and dump. Back and forth, yank and dump.

I was grabbing my last wad of clothes when I felt the now familiar sensation of hot and cold, prickles and goose bumps. And then,

smack in the middle
of my clothes, an-
other vision ap-
peared. This time,
here's what I saw:

An upside-down
   ostrich

Huh?! Getting
my room ready for
Aunt Jenna would
have to wait. I needed to talk to Elizabeth.

I had just started to call her back when Dad
appeared in my doorway, carrying the vacuum
and a bucket of cleaning supplies. He was coming to help me clean my room and we didn't finish until it was too late to call my best friend
with an update.

I guess my room wasn't as clean as I had
thought.

Friday morning Elizabeth was at the bus stop first. When I got there she looked me up and down like she had never seen a human person before in her life.

"Why are you dressed like that?" she demanded.

Okay, here's the deal. All of my clothes were still in a messy heap on Milo's floor, so this morning when I overslept and got dressed in a hurry, I grabbed the first things I could find in the pile, which turned out to be a stained sweatshirt with unicorns on it and bright pink sweatpants that I've never worn in public. So, yes, I may have looked a little strange.

Comfy. But strange.

"Never mind," I said as I saw the bus slowly turning the corner, making its way onto our street. "I had another vision!" I whispered.

After we climbed onto the bus and slid into empty side-by-side seats in the third row, I told Elizabeth about the upside-down ostrich.

Elizabeth said, "That is a head-scratcher," and then actually scratched her head in thought.

I agreed. Since we do not usually come across animals at our school, especially of the extremely-large-bird variety, I suggested that Elizabeth take out a pencil and paper so we could write down all the possible explanations.

Here's what we came up with:

> 1. An ostrich has escaped from the zoo and is going to show up in our classroom.
> 2. We will be taking a surprise field trip to an ostrich farm.
> 3. Someone is bringing an ostrich for show-and-tell.
> 4. I am going to be attacked by an ostrich.

To be honest, none of these seemed likely possibilities, but by the time we pulled up to school, that's what we had.

Now we just needed to see if any of our theories were right.

• • • • •

In class that morning, we were supposed to be doing a worksheet of multiplication problems, but I was using my colored pencils to draw a picture of an ostrich on a piece of scratch paper. I thought maybe if I could draw the picture from my vision, it might be easier to figure out what it meant. Besides, I already knew how to multiply.

"Time's up, everyone!" Mrs. Agnes announced.

I snapped my head up. *What?* For real live?"

"Yes, Hazel, for real live," Mrs. Agnes said with a heavy sigh as dramatic as my mom's.

"But that was so short!" I said.

"Well, we're stopping a little early today because I have a special announcement," she said in a singsongy voice. "Papers to the front, please."

I scribbled down the answer to the last math

problem as everyone else passed their work forward. Mrs. Agnes came to the back row and collected my paper.

She took one look and raised her eyebrows. "Twenty-eight times nine equals 'toes'?"

"It says 205!" I protested.

She fixed her eyes on me. "Well, perhaps we need to work on our handwriting. And our math, because the answer is 252."

Now it was my turn to sigh. Then I went back to my ostrich drawing.

Mrs. Agnes collected all the papers and put them on her desk next to a giant fabric apple that a student gave her as a gift, I'm guessing about five million years ago because there was a huge rip all the way across the top and the stem had fallen off. Then she turned to us, her expression suddenly sunny. "Okay, everyone. I didn't want to say anything before I knew for certain . . ."

I kept drawing, half paying attention.

"But I've been trying to get these performers for the Spring Spectacular for *years* now. And finally, I did! I really, really did!" Mrs. Agnes sounded extremely pleased with herself, as if she just ended world hunger instead of finding a dumb act for the school carnival.

I looked down at my drawing. I guess the ostrich in my vision had a lot more feathers than ostriches usually have, because without thinking, I had drawn a bird with about a million colorful feathers arranged in a really cool pattern. I couldn't imagine what kind of ostrich looked like that. Suddenly, I considered another possibility, one that Elizabeth and I hadn't thought of on the bus: *Maybe it wasn't an ostrich at all.* Because now that I was looking at it closely, the ostrich almost looked more like a person . . . or

even . . . people? . . .
yes, people. People
dressed in colorful
feathers . . . costumes!
But why would they be
hanging upside down?

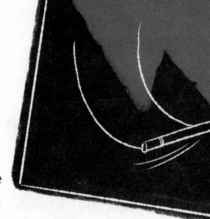

"The special performers will be—" Mrs. Agnes was saying.

Performers? That's when it hit me, like a trapeze artist falling out of the sky and onto my head.

"Acrobats!" I yelled, staring at my drawing. "It's a troupe of acrobats! With purple and red feathers, and gold headpieces, and they flip and swing upside down, and behind them is a backdrop with a lightning bolt on it!"

I smiled triumphantly.

Then I noticed everyone was staring at me.

Lila tilted her head at me. "Don't be silly, Hazy. Mrs. Agnes didn't even tell us anything yet."

But Mrs. Agnes was looking at me from the front of the classroom with squinty, suspicious eyes. "Actually, Lila, Hazel is right. About all of it." She took a poster from her desk drawer and held it up:

Acrobats. Purple and red feathers. Gold headpieces. Swinging upside down. Backdrop with a lightning bolt. Just like my vision.

From her seat right next to me, Elizabeth was looking my way with the biggest grin I've ever seen.

9

"Do you know what you have? Tomorrow power."

Elizabeth and I were walking home from the bus stop after school.

"Whatty what, now?" I said absently. I was very busy pretending that I had just arrived on Mars and had to watch my step or I would fall headfirst into Mariner Valley, which is this crazy thing four times as deep as the Grand Canyon.

"Pay attention, Hazy Bloom!" Elizabeth said.

I paid attention, even if it meant falling off the edge of the planet.

"Think about it. Every time you have a vision, it comes true the next day."

I didn't say anything.

"The day after you have it."

I still didn't say anything.

Elizabeth spoke very slowly. "And *tomorrow* is what we call the day after—"

"I know what tomorrow is!" I retorted. The truth is, I was thinking it over to see if she was right. I quickly recalled my visions. The food fight, the number on Lila's shirt, the ostrich that was really an acrobatic troupe—all of those things happened for real live the day after I saw them in my head.

"Tomorrow power," I said, testing out how the words sounded. I kind of liked it.

But I'm pretty sure Elizabeth liked it more, because she was now hopping up and down on the curb like nobody's business. "My best friend has tomorrow power!" she chirped. *"My best friend has tomorrow power!"*

Our fourth-grade neighbor Jarrod passed by on his scooter and looked at us funny.

I lowered my voice even though Elizabeth was the one shouting. "Okay, let's just calm down—"

But she kept right on going. "Do you think you have other powers, too? Maybe you can fly! Or breathe underwater!"

"I cannot breathe underwater."

"You could be a superhero!"

"A superhero? Really?" I perked up, suddenly intrigued. Then I smacked into a mailbox.

Elizabeth stared at me. "Unlikely. But possible."

Fine, I'm a little clumsy. I get it from my dad.

"But you definitely have tomorrow power," Elizabeth said proudly, as if she had arranged the whole thing.

I smiled. "Maybe Milo will be nicer to me now, after I tell him."

Elizabeth stopped and grabbed me by the wrists.

"Hazy Bloom, you can't tell anyone about this."

First I said, "Ouch!" Then I said, "Why not?"

"Because!"

If you ask me, that didn't sound like a very convincing reason.

She went on. "Superheroes—and you *might* be a superhero—must keep their identities a secret!"

"Or what?"

"Or it could be a disaster! Remember what happened when everyone found out Mark Kent was Batman?"

I crossed my arms. "It's *Clark* Kent and he was *Super*man," I said. Obviously, I knew a little more about superheroes than Elizabeth did. It helped to have an older sibling with a giant comic book collection sometimes. Other times it didn't help, like when that older sibling lets out a huge burp and then pretends it was you. The point is, Elizabeth should get an older brother or sister. And also, she had a lot to learn about superheroes.

"Fine, whatever," she said.
"Just remember. *No one* can
know."

"You know."

"That's because I'm your sidekick."

"Says who?" I didn't get to choose my own sidekick? I was offended. "I think I should be able to choose my own sidekick, Elizabeth."

"Okay . . ." Elizabeth tapped her foot impatiently, like she was dealing with a small, uncooperative child. "Who do you choose for your sidekick?"

I paused. "You."

"Good, it's settled. Oh, do we need a secret signal? Yes, we do! To warn each other about stuff."

I giggled. Elizabeth was really getting into it. Okay, this was kind of fun.

As I waved goodbye to Elizabeth and walked to my house, I let myself imagine for a moment that I had tomorrow power and was a possible superhero. Maybe I'd use my powers to fight evil and prevent a horrible tragedy like a fire, or getting mango in my fruit salad. Maybe I'd save one hundred people from doom and they'd give me a medal and a parade (I bet they would also donate money to my Mars mission!). I'd get to be on TV, and sign autographs, and probably not have to do my spelling homework. Who has time for spelling when you're busy preventing doom?

That's when I saw my mom standing on the porch. Arms crossed. Toe tapping.

She didn't look happy to see a possibly real-live superhero.

10

"Hazel, we got a call this afternoon from Mrs. Agnes," Mom said. She had ushered me into the living room and plopped me on the couch.

Dad was already home from work. He was standing across from me with a stern look on his face. Between you and me, I liked tripping-over-the-dog Dad a lot better than looking-at-me-sternly Dad.

"That's weird," I replied.

"She said there was an incident today about . . . acrobats?"

Uh-oh.

Dad spoke. "Mrs. Agnes seems to believe you were snooping in her desk."

"What? I didn't do that!"

From the other room, I heard "Ooooooooooooooooooh!" It was Milo practicing his ghost noises for the haunted house. His impression really needed some work. He sounded like a wounded cow.

Mom continued, "Mrs. Agnes told me that she had a poster that no one could have seen

because it was hidden in her desk, but that you described it perfectly before she had even showed it. Can you explain that?"

I couldn't believe Mrs. Agnes thought I was snooping! Just because I was right about the acrobats and the color of their costumes and that they were swinging upside down, and that there was a backdrop of a lightning bolt, and . . .

Okay, I could maybe see why she thought I was snooping.

Mom's expression turned softer. "Hazel, is there anything you want to talk to us about?"

Dad added, "You can tell us anything, sweetie."

I considered telling them about my visions. What would be the big deal? They'd probably be excited for me. Maybe they'd even tell Milo I was now in charge, and would excuse me from all my chores due to my superhero duties.

Or . . . they'd get worried and take me to the

doctor. Then maybe the doctor would think I had an overactive imagination and was just seeking attention due to poor self-esteem, and Mom would sign me up for kung fu because Jarrod the neighbor did it and it did wonders for his confidence, according to what his mom told my mom, except now Jarrod is super-irritating because he walks through the hallways doing all these ninja moves. The point is, I always used to enjoy the song "Kung Fu Fighting" but not anymore. Also, I wasn't ready to talk to my par-

ents about my visions. But . . . was there another way to tell them?

I thought of our unit in Language Arts last
month on metaphors, which is when you're
talking about one thing but you really mean
something else.

I'd try it.

"Mom, Dad," I began slowly. "Do you know
how sometimes people get warts, and then the
warts go away, but sometimes they come back
again? And it's kind of interesting and exciting,
but it can also cause problems like getting in
trouble with your teacher?"

I think that's how metaphors work.

My parents were quiet for a minute. Then
Dad said, "Hazy, do you have a wart?"

"What? No!"

"If you do, we can make an appointment
with Dr. Rogers."

"Dad, I don't have a wart!"

"They're very easy to remove. Unless it's in a tricky place like—"

"I DO NOT HAVE A WART."

Maybe I hadn't chosen the best metaphor.

Milo came in, being annoying just by *walking into the room*, which was pretty impressive, in a way. "What's all the yelling for? Ooh, is Hazy in *trouble*?"

"No!" I said before Mom could shush him, and I stomped off down the hall. I wished Milo would get a wart.

Mom called after me: "Mrs. Agnes wants to talk to you on Monday and I expect you to explain yourself and apologize, young lady!"

Great. I didn't want to talk to Mrs. Agnes. I didn't need to apologize for anything! I hadn't snooped. I'd had a vision!

I just wanted to go to my room and *be alone*. Mom was now yelling to me about something else, but by that point I was already down the hall and couldn't hear her. I flung my door open.

"Hazel Hillary Bloom!" a chipper voice rang out. Sitting on my bed, grinning from ear to ear, was Aunt Jenna. I'd forgotten she was coming today. Just great.

11

Aunt Jenna stood up, and I suddenly remembered how tall she was. Tall and skinny, with a long neck and black wavy hair falling over her eyes. She looked like a giraffe with bangs. Her long purple skirt swished from side to side as she walked toward me.

"Look at you, you're getting soooo big! Aw, come here. Give your aunt a hug."

She grabbed me in a tight squeeze. I sort of gently patted her back like she was a dog. I didn't know her too well.

But Aunt Jenna didn't seem to mind. She pulled away and looked at me with smiling eyes. "Thank you *so* much for letting me sleep in your room, Hazy Bloom."

I almost said, *I didn't let you, my mom made me,* but instead I mumbled, "You're welcome." But I wanted to say the first thing. Even though she did call me by my preferred name. My mom must have told her I liked that.

Then she did an excited little bounce. "Oh! I brought you something."

From her duffel bag, Aunt Jenna carefully produced a large, square cardboard box and held it out to me. I opened it and peered inside.

"Huh," I said.

"They're rain boots!" she exclaimed giddily, as if she'd invented the concept herself.

See what I mean? Kooky gift! It practically *never* rains in Denver, so it didn't make any

sense to get some very
green, sort-of-ugly rain
boots as a gift.

"Wow," I said, try-
ing to be enthusiastic.
"Thanks, Aunt Jenna."

To show her how
much I appreciated
the thought, I made
a big deal of putting
them on. Then I told Aunt Jenna I was going to
take a nap before dinner, grabbed my favorite
pillow from my bed, and slumped down the hall
into Milo's room. As I walked through the door,
a spitball hit me in the forehead.

"Hi, dorkface," Milo said.

I slammed out of the room and went to try
to find a place where I could lie down and be
angry for a little bit without anyone bothering
me.

12

I had the worst Friday night in the history of ever. For one thing, Milo sleeps sideways and therefore kicked me in the legs all night long. I don't know when he started sleeping sideways or why he sleeps sideways, or if he even knows he sleeps sideways. The point is, I woke up cranky and with sore shins. This weekend was off to a bad start.

Then it got worse. Mom insisted that we show Aunt Jenna around town, which was boring and wet because Saturday's the day it finally decided to rain. Every time we crossed a street, I was the one who stepped in a puddle. Whenever a car drove past, I was the one who got splashed. At least I had my new rain boots to keep me from getting totally soaked. But it didn't make the day any better.

Things didn't improve on Sunday. Milo was still sleeping sideways and had now added snoring to his obnoxious nighttime habits. Plus, Sunday meant it was one day closer to Monday, which meant apologizing to Mrs. Agnes about the snooping I did not do.

Then at dinner, The Baby bit me. What did I ever do to him?

By Sunday night, I was ready to declare this the WWEFRL ("worst weekend ever, for real live"). Dad, Milo, and I were watching a movie about a talking horse that Milo and Dad thought was hilarious but I thought was the dumbest thing on the planet (and I'm pretty sure Mr. Cheese agreed with me because he left the room as soon as it started). Then it happened.

Prickles and goose bumps. Hot and cold. Another vision.

A man in a checkered shirt,

sitting at a desk.

I focused as hard as I could on the vision before I knew it would flash away. On the desk was a giant, torn-up fabric apple. Mrs. Agnes's desk! But the man wasn't Mrs. Agnes. Obviously. So who was he?

"Ryan, do you have any sugar substitute for my tea?" Aunt Jenna poked her head out of the kitchen to ask my Dad.

Substitute?

Dad paused the movie and hopped up to get her some. Meanwhile, I had just figured out who the man in the checkered shirt was. He was a substitute teacher! In my classroom! Which meant, tomorrow—no Mrs. Agnes, no apologizing, and no getting in trouble. Woohoo! Best. Vision. Ever!

I leaped up from the couch and twirled around happily. I started jumping up and down, cracking up The Baby. Then I started jumping up and down *with* The Baby. Then I put him down and boogied across the family room carpet and onto the kitchen floor (very slippery, I do not recommend), and after picking myself up from my second or third fall I ended with a celebratory jump. As you might have guessed, I was pretty excited.

Aunt Jenna laughed and said there was a word for my mood, which was *jubilant*, a word I instantly loved. I repeated it over and over. "Jubilant, jubilant. J-u-b-i-l-a-n-t!"

I had to call Elizabeth and tell her right away about my tomorrow vision.

Unfortunately, Elizabeth's mom said my sidekick couldn't talk because she was busy ex-

perimenting with cupcake recipes for the contest, and how was my cupcake research coming?

Oops.

It was possible Elizabeth was going to be a
little bit mad that according to her detailed plan,
this weekend I was supposed to be finding the
best cupcake recipe and instead I was, well, not.
But then I decided
maybe she'd be so
happy about the
substitute thing
that she'd forget
all about it.

13

The next day, Monday, Milo's alarm blared so loudly it knocked me out of his bed and onto the floor. He was still sound asleep. I was thinking about hiding his underwear in the freezer to get him back when I remembered the substitute. And I instantly felt a hundred times better. I got dressed from the pile of clothes on the floor, and it wasn't until I was washing my face in the bathroom that I got a good look at what I'd put on, which was a stretchy yellow skirt I hadn't worn since first grade and my brother's Pokémon hoodie (how did that end up with my stuff?). It didn't matter. Today was going to be great!

At school, I eagerly peeked in the doorway of our class-room looking for the sub-stitute. He wasn't there yet. I skipped down the hall to tell Elizabeth the news, but as soon as she saw me, she insisted on speaking first.

"We need to discuss your clothing situation," she said.

"I'm living in my brother's room!" I said defensively. "But anyway, guess what?" I said. "We're having a substitute today! For real live!"

"How do you know?" asked Lila, who I guess had overheard me.

"Yeah, how do you know?" Mapefrl said, drifting toward us. "Did Mrs. Agnes call you and tell you?" he asked sarcastically.

"No. But trust me. I have my ways of knowing." I winked at Elizabeth, because *she* knew how I knew.

"Hazy Bloom, what's wrong with your eye?" Elizabeth said.

Okay, fine. I don't know how to wink.

Mapefrl was clearly trying to be extra-annoying today because then he said, "Fine. If you say there's a sub, prove it."

"Prove it how?" I didn't like where this was going.

"Play a prank on the sub," he said.

I gulped. I have never played a prank on anyone before, unless you count

distracting The Baby so I could eat his graham crackers or putting toothpaste in my brother's soccer shoes. (But I only did that once. Okay, three times.) I certainly have never played a prank at school. Or on a grown-up.

So I said, "No way, buster. Not doing it."

Mapefrl smirked. "I knew it. You'd never do anything like that. You're too *scared*."

Okay, here was the thing: I wasn't going to take that from Mapefrl. I wasn't scared and I was going to prove it. Besides, the good news about playing a prank on a sub was that you couldn't get in trouble with your teacher because they weren't there, hence the sub (spelling word:

hence, not *sub*). I snuck into the empty classroom and put together a prank plan. First, I was going to turn all the student desks backward. Then I would open all the windows. Then I'd flip on the radio in the back of the classroom so rock music would start blaring. Then I would take some old gummy fish from the bottom of my backpack and stick them on the teacher's chair.

I started putting my plan into action and turned the first desk around. *This'll show Mape-frl. It will be the best prank in the history of ever.*

Then Mrs. Agnes walked in.

Uh-oh. For real live.

• • • • •

Here's a question.

How was I supposed to know that Mrs. Agnes *was* going to be there today, and that later in the morning her computer screen

would go haywire and since the regular computer guy, Mr. Tennison, was on vacation in Aruba, a *new* computer guy who none of us knew would come in to fix her screen, and *he was the one in the checkered shirt* sitting at her desk in my vision?

Also, where is Aruba? I wonder if it's near Mozambique.

I almost asked Mrs. Agnes but then thought better of it. The other kids had gone out for recess and she had just had a "little chat" with me about my supposedly snooping in her desk the other day and my attempted prank. I apologized like I was supposed to but I could tell she didn't believe me. Then she gave me a "very stern warning" and said I'd better choose my actions from now on "very carefully" because I was on "very thin ice." I wasn't sure what ice had to do with my thinking there'd be a substitute, or why she was even talking about ice because it was spring. And then her comments reminded me about my ice-skating rink on Mars and how I'll definitely need an effective advertising campaign to attract customers (Hey, I guess the word *campaign* does come up after all!).

The point is, this was all my tomorrow power's fault. If I hadn't had any visions to begin with, my teacher wouldn't be accusing me of being a snoop and I wouldn't have wrongly thought there was a sub. For the first time, I wished the visions would just stop for a little while. Lately they had been causing nothing but trouble. Plus, Elizabeth kept reminding me about our cupcake plan and how we needed to stay on schedule because it's "our dream" (her dream) to go to theater camp and therefore we *must* win. Great. Now on top of everything else, I had two days to get organized to make fifty cupcakes from scratch.

The one bright spot was that I was the only one in my class who got the bonus word right on our surprise spelling test: *jubilant*.

14

After the substitute-who-wasn't-a-substitute fiasco, I had no more visions for three whole days, and that was just fine with me. I used that time to get back on track with my space mission, break in my new rain boots (I actually kind of liked them now), and make cupcakes for the bake sale.

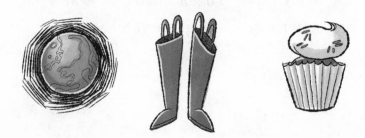

Well, by "make cupcakes," I mean that I took some of the ingredients from the pantry. The actual making part was what I forgot to do. I didn't mean to forget, it's just that on my way to get Mom so she could help me, I got distracted by an urgent matter, which was choosing an email address that I could check from Mars (Dad said I could get my own account when I turned ten, and who knows how long I'll be up there hanging out in space? Especially if my ice-skating business takes off). The point is, I decided on the following: hazybloomisonmars @onmarsforreallive.com. Also, I completely forgot about the cupcakes.

Suddenly, it was Wednesday night, and according to Elizabeth's plan, we had to bring all our cupcakes to school the next day. Only, I had zero cupcakes to bring. And I couldn't even quickly throw some together from a boxed mix

(you do remember that rule, right? I hope so, for your own sake). I had a feeling Elizabeth was not going to be pleased.

• • • • •

"You didn't make *any* cupcakes? None?" Elizabeth bellowed from her desk the next morning. I hadn't seen her until now because Dad had driven Milo and me to school on account of us running a little late, which was completely Milo's fault.

Fine, it was my fault. I wanted to wear my

purple stripy shirt and had to look all over the house ten times before finally discovering it wadded up in The Baby's diaper drawer. Seriously, who puts away stuff in our house? The point is, Elizabeth was furious, just as I'd predicted.

"Today is Thursday," she whispered angrily because now Mrs. Agnes was handing out worksheets for our science unit on emperor penguins. "The carnival is *Saturday*! How are we supposed to make a cupcake tower without all the cupcakes? We can't, that's how!"

"I'm sorry," I mumbled. "It's just, I was work-

ing on my space mission and then I got another vision and—"

"You got another vision?" Elizabeth's expression went from angry and huffy to curious and maybe a little crazy, then landed right back on mad. It was fascinating. "Why didn't you tell me?" she demanded.

"Because . . . I've been waiting for you to stop yelling at me?" I thought a little witty humor might calm her down. It didn't.

She leaned forward and spoke to me like every word was a separate, important piece of information. "You. Need. To. Tell. Me. Every. Vision. Do you think you can figure out these things all on your own? Well, you cannot!"

Mrs. Agnes snapped her fingers at us, then stared at me extra-hard to remind me about my very thin ice.

We were quiet for a minute, not just because of Mrs. Agnes but because I was waiting for

Elizabeth to decide which emotion she'd like to go with next. Finally she gave me a tiny smile. "So? Tell me about the vision. What did you see?"

Ha! She just had to know. It's like they say: "curiosity fed the cat when you let it out of the bag." At least I think that's what they say, although someone should tell them it makes absolutely no sense. Also, who are "they"?

Anyway, I answered her. "Eggs," I said. "That's what I saw. A carton of eggs."

"Interesting," Elizabeth said, even though a carton of eggs was the most uninteresting thing I could think of in the whole world, for real live. "I wonder what it means?"

I wondered the same thing. The vision had come just as I was drifting off to sleep last night, and I had been sure it meant we would be having eggs for breakfast. But this morning when I'd asked, Mom had said we were all out.

So really, when else would I see eggs? I told all of this to Elizabeth, who nodded very thoughtfully but then just said, "Hm."

In my opinion, *hm* is not a very sidekick-y thing to say, but that's just me.

But then, Elizabeth pointed out the window, a slow smile forming. "I think I solved your egg mystery," she said.

There, in the athletic field behind our school, a group of fifth graders were starting to set up for the Spring Spectacular. At the far end, three kids were unloading a bunch of egg cartons from a giant crate onto a small red wagon. One of the kids was holding a sign: EGG TOSS.

In case you don't know what an egg toss is, it's a game where you throw an egg back and forth with someone and try not to break it or you'll get gooey egg yolk all over the place, which has never happened to me because I am an excellent egg tosser. (I mean *egg*-cellent egg tosser. Ha-ha.) The point is, I was suddenly in the mood for an omelet. Also, my vision was now making a little more sense. I had found the eggs. But what *about* them? Was there going to be an egg accident? An egg emergency? I hadn't wanted another vision, but now that it had happened, I needed to find out what it was all about. After all, it was kind of my job as a possible superhero.

"Hazel and Elizabeth,

please get away from the window and back to your desks," Mrs. Agnes snapped. I turned to her.

"Mrs. Agnes, may I have a hall pass? Bathroom."

Elizabeth looked at me, alarmed. "What are you doing?" she asked.

"Preventing doom," I said, all superhero-y.

"Now?"

"Yuppers," I said.

"You can't!" Elizabeth insisted. "You could get in big trouble, Hazy Bloom. And I don't want anything getting in the way of us winning the cupcake contest and going to theater camp. It's our dream!"

(Her dream.)

Anyway, I'm not exactly proud of this, but here's what I did next: I ignored my sidekick. Maybe I was growing into my superhero role, but at that moment I knew something was going to happen with the eggs, and it was up to me, Hazy Bloom, to figure out what it was and how to stop it.

Also, I really did have to go to the bathroom.

15

I crept out of the girls' bathroom and looked up and down the hallway. Empty. Time to make my move.

I ran toward the door that led outside to the field. I hesitated—was I making a mistake? I didn't want to do anything to get in trouble again and fall through the very thin ice— whatever that meant. On the other hand, I knew that I had to take drastic steps to prevent doom.

I pushed open the door and made my way over to the three kids, who had just finished unloading the last egg carton onto the wagon. I could now see that one of the kids was Milo's friend Kingston, who was like the fifth-grade version of Mapefrl (I call him Fgvomapefrl). Here's why: instead of helping the other two kids stack the eggs, or arrange the eggs, or pull the wagon with the eggs, or do anything helpful with the eggs, Kingston was pretending to crack the eggs over another kid's head.

When he saw me, he called out: "Hey, Milo's sister! Only fifth graders allowed!"

Their teacher came over. "Young lady? Shouldn't you be in Mrs. Agnes's classroom?"

I thought fast. "Oh, yeah, but we're doing a science lesson and . . . um, we needed some . . . dirt." I pointed to the ground.

"Oh, what's the lesson about?" the teacher asked with interest.

I paused. "Penguins," I said. I have no clue why anyone would need dirt for a lesson on penguins. But it was all I could think of.

I bent down and scooped up a handful of dirt, then realized I had nothing to put it in, so I just stuck it in my pants pocket.

The teacher arched an eyebrow. Then she carried on with the carnival setup.

Kingston was now bothering a girl painting a ticket booth by dangling an egg over her head. I remembered that girl from a project she once did with Milo. She was nice.

"Stop it," the girl was saying, waving him away with her paintbrush.

"*Stop it!*" Kingston mimicked. He might be even more annoying than the original Mapefrl, and that's saying a lot. The other two kids were totally encouraging him, too. Or maybe I should say, "egging him on," ha-ha. Okay, fine, this was no time for jokes.

The teacher told Kingston to "cool it" and he finally stopped *tormenting* (spelling word) the poor girl and got back to his actual job of pulling the wagon. They were now headed up the small but steep grassy hill in the middle of the field that in kindergarten I called "Roly-Poly Guacamole" because first of all, it was fun to roll down, and second of all, I was really into Mexican food at the time. But now there were three annoying boys pulling a wagon of eggs up it. At least the nice girl was safely back to painting.

The teacher told the kids she was going inside to get some supplies, and as soon as she did, the boys dropped the handle of the wagon right there at the top of the hill. Then, Kingston popped open an egg carton and he and his friends started throwing eggs back and forth.

Kingston had his back to the wagon, and the other two kids had run down to the bottom. With each throw, Kingston inched closer to the wagon, which, may I remind you, was stuffed with cartons of raw eggs. One slip, and he would send the wagon careening straight back down the hill . . . right into the nice girl's ticket booth.

"Pop-up!" called one of the boys from the bottom of the hill, flinging an egg high into the air. The other boy cackled as Kingston took a giant step backward, his arms stretched up, and I knew this was it. He was going to knock the wagon down the hill and into the ticket booth—and I couldn't let that happen. So I did what any superhero would do in this situation.

I screamed. "Noooooooooooooooooooo!" Then I closed my eyes, waiting for the sound of a wagon crashing and eggs exploding everywhere.

But there was no crash. No exploding. Instead, I opened my eyes and saw Kingston staring at me. He was holding the egg the other kid had thrown. I guess he'd caught it after all.

Which means I got another vision wrong.

"What is wrong with you?" he yelled. The other kids were now looking at me, too, with *bewilderment*

117

(spelling word but not really the point in this humiliating moment).

I stammered, trying to figure out what to say.

That's when I heard loud, angry knocks coming from inside a classroom. *My* classroom. I squinted and saw Mrs. Agnes standing at the window, gesturing angrily for me to get inside.

I believe I had just fallen through the very thin ice.

16

As a consequence of sneaking outside during class, I was taken off the bake sale and put on the cleanup crew with Mapefrl. I also had to stay inside during recess, which was completely unfair.

I watched through the window as everyone else ran around having fun while I sat inside with Mrs. Agnes and her dumb fabric apple. I turned to her. "Mrs. Agnes, I'm sorry I snuck outside during science, but it was to prevent doom, for real live!"

"Doom?" Mrs. Agnes looked at me like I was a Martian, even though I, of all people, understand that Martians are completely fictional. She was clearly not interested in my excuses.

Then there was the issue of Elizabeth. "Didn't I tell you not to go outside this morning, Hazy Bloom? Yes, I did!" she blustered later at lunch when I finally got out of my prison sentence with Mrs. Agnes. "Now . . . it's just me!" she said, pointing to herself to remind us who "me" was. "How am I supposed to finish making the cupcakes, decorate them all, and arrange every single one around the cupcake tower so they're perfectly spaced and attractive from all angles, all by myself? It's impossible!" She pushed away her lunch tray in a huff.

I looked at my friend. Elizabeth wanted to win that contest so badly. Now she wouldn't win or go to theater camp. All because of me. I felt terrible.

Then I felt mad. But not at Elizabeth. At my tomorrow power. Between getting accused of

snooping, mistaking the computer guy for a substitute, and trying to prevent egg doom when there was no doom, it seemed like all my power did lately was get me in trouble. What had started out as fun and exciting was becoming a great big *aggravation* (spelling word). In fact, it was ruining everything. I was fed up.

That's why right then, I made a decision: *No. More. Visions.* I would stay so busy, there wouldn't be time for a vision to pop into my head. And if one did, I'd be so busy I wouldn't even notice. All I had to do was stay busy, busy, busy.

· · · · ·

Staying busy is harder than it sounds.

At lunch, I tried to help my friends clear their trays, but they thought I was trying to start another food fight and wouldn't let me. In class, I tried to help Mrs. Agnes hand out our division homework, but when I went up to her desk she thought I was trying to snoop again (even though I hadn't done it before) and made me sit down.

At home it didn't get any easier. As Mom and Aunt Jenna got ready for a "girls' night out," I offered to teach The Baby to jump rope, but did you know that babies cannot do this? I mean, how hard is *jumping*? I needed another way to stay busy.

Here's what I did for the rest of the afternoon:

1. Braided my hair into seven parts.
2. Learned to wiggle my ears.
3. Made up a new dance move called the Hazy Bloom Jazz Lunge.
4. Tried to mind-control my fish.
5. Made a schedule for my first three days in space.
6. Tried to look happy, angry, and puzzled at the same time.
7. Spun around super-duper fast in my mom's desk chair even though she always tells me not to because I'll get hurt.
8. Got hurt.

That evening, I was trying to figure out
something else to do to stay busy when Dad
walked through the kitchen
door carrying two paper
bags. "Hey there, Hazel
Basil. Help me unload
these groceries?"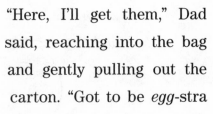

Bingo!

"Sure," I chirped, and
beelined over to him.

I started unloading the
groceries at record speed.

Dad pointed to one of
the bags. "Careful with that
one. There are eggs in there."

Eggs?

 "Here, I'll get them," Dad
said, reaching into the bag
and gently pulling out the
carton. "Got to be *egg*-stra

careful with these guys," he said with a wink. We totally have the same sense of humor.

Then he tripped over Mr. Cheese and the eggs went flying and, well, you can picture the rest.

I had finally figured out yesterday's vision.

The good news is, cleaning up the icky egg mess was a great way to stay busy, busy, busy. Even if it was totally disgusting.

17

By Friday afternoon, I felt *victorious* (not a spelling word but I heard it on a TV commercial and enjoy saying it). I had managed to keep any visions from popping into my head for almost two whole days. It was nice to feel in control of my tomorrow power.

I plopped down on the couch next to Mr. Cheese and watched Milo flip the channels between a reality fishing show and a sitcom about triplets. Aunt Jenna was sitting on the floor playing patty-cake with The Baby while Mom skimmed through a magazine. She seemed happy to have her sister around.

Milo found another show and was now flipping back and forth between all three. I was about to yell at him to make up his mind when I felt it.

Arms prickly.

Goose bumps.

Hot and cold. *Nuts.*

It was another vision.

"No!" I shouted, trying to make it go away.

"No, what?" Mom said.

"Nothing," I said quickly. I wished it were nothing. But before I could stop it, there it was, flashing through my head, a blur of colors, shapes, and lines all jumbled together:

Rainbow bubbles...

green sparkles...

a falling object, and...

a fluffy pink cat?

None of it made sense. Except for one thing. If I was getting this vision today, then whatever it was about would happen tomorrow.

And tomorrow was the Spring Spectacular.

"Mom," I said urgently as I stood up. "I need to go to Elizabeth's."

"Now? Why?" Mom asked. "Dad'll be home soon with takeout."

"But—but I need to tell her something!" I stammered.

"Can't you just call her?"

"No, it's too important! Bubbles! Green stuff! Fluffy cat!"

I sounded like I had lost it.

Mom studied me with concern. "Hazel, what's gotten into you? You have been acting so strange lately."

"Yeah," said Milo. "Even weirder than usual."

Aunt Jenna was looking at me, too, with an odd expression somewhere between a smile and a frown. It made me feel uneasy.

Now Mom was inching closer to me. "Tell us what's going on."

"Yeah, tell us," echoed Milo.

The Baby was getting fussy and Aunt Jenna pulled him onto her lap.

The room was feeling smaller. They knew I was hiding something, and they wanted answers. Was this the right time to tell them? Would they even believe me? Would they think I was crazy? Would it ruin everything, like Elizabeth said? I gulped, not knowing what to do. I felt trapped.

Then, from Aunt Jenna's lap, The Baby said: "Blah-blah beefrechenutz."

Look, I don't know what *beefrechenutz* means to you, because to me it sounds like

BEEFRECHENUTZ

someone spitting out cheese puffs. But at that moment, Mom whirled around and stared at The Baby in amazement.

"Oh my goodness," she marveled. "He just said his first word!" Everyone turned to look.

This was my chance to escape. "Be back in a jiff!" I chirped and ran for the door.

On the way to Elizabeth's I felt a surge of relief knowing my sidekick would help me think through my vision and figure it all out. I couldn't wait to see her.

But when Elizabeth opened the door, she didn't look like she was in sidekick mode. For one thing, she was covered in flour. "Hazy Bloom, what are you doing here?" she said, kind of not nicely.

Words started flying out of my mouth. "I just had another vision about the Spack Spring-tacular! I mean, the Sping Spricktacular! You

130

know what I mean. Anyway, I saw a bunch of green sparkly stuff, some kind of rainbow-bubble thingy, and another thing falling down, I'm not sure what it was. Oh, and a pink fluffy cat! Seriously, that one has me stumped. So what do you think?" I looked at her, anxious for her answer.

And then Elizabeth looked at me and said, "I'm sorry, Hazy Bloom, but I can't help you right now."

I looked at her in disbelief. "But—but this is important!"

"I know, but we were right in the middle of—"

"We? Who's we?"

"Hi, Hazy," a voice called.

It was May.

"What's she doing here?" I said. I realized that didn't sound very polite. But I wasn't feeling very polite because my sidekick was making me mad.

Elizabeth pointed to May. "She's my new partner for the cupcake contest."

131

"*What?*" I said very loudly.

"You're on the cleanup crew now," she said, like I didn't know that.

"But—I need your help!"

Elizabeth looked at me with squinty eyes. "Well, I needed *your* help for the cupcake contest. And you didn't help at all! You did *nothing*!"

I glared at her. "Excuse me for being a little busy with *my new superpower*! That *you* were more excited about than me!"

"Well, not anymore!" Elizabeth said, all huffy.

132

"That's it. You're *so* not my sidekick anymore."

"Fine!" Elizabeth yelled.

"Fine!"

"Fine!"

May whispered, "I'll go check on the batter," and tiptoed away. It's possible she was slightly confused by our conversation.

But it didn't matter because I was already storming away back to my house. I was furious. Elizabeth couldn't just decide to stop being my sidekick because of some stupid bake-sale cupcakes. How dare she! She knew how important my tomorrow power was! I guessed she just didn't care anymore.

I stomped back home to find Aunt Jenna sitting outside on the front porch.

Between you and me, she was the last person I wanted to see. Except for Elizabeth, because I never wanted to see her again. Well, and Milo. And Mapefrl. And Mrs. Agnes. And The Baby, depending on my mood. But after all those people, definitely Aunt Jenna.

Yet there she was, her head tilted up toward the sky, emitting some kind of strange gurgling, singing noise from the back of her throat.

I was still furious, but seriously? That was just too weird to ignore. "What are you doing?" I asked her.

"Birdcalls. Want to learn?"

"No thanks," I said.

But instead of walking past her into the house, I sat down next to her. I don't know why, I just did. We sat there together for a while in silence, which was actually quite peaceful and calm. Then it got really boring.

"Fine, I'll learn," I said.

So over the next half hour, while we waited for Dad to get home with dinner, Aunt Jenna

taught me the art of birdcalling. At first I felt silly, but after I got the hang of it, I was gurgling and singing as loud as can be. Soon, we were having a hilarious birdcall conversation that ended with both of us cracking up so hard we fell onto our backs laughing. It was fun. And it definitely got my mind off Elizabeth. At least for a little while.

I turned and smiled. "Thanks, Aunt Jenna."

"You're welcome, Hazy Bloom," she said. I decided Aunt Jenna wasn't so bad after all. Although I don't know why you'd ever want to call a bird.

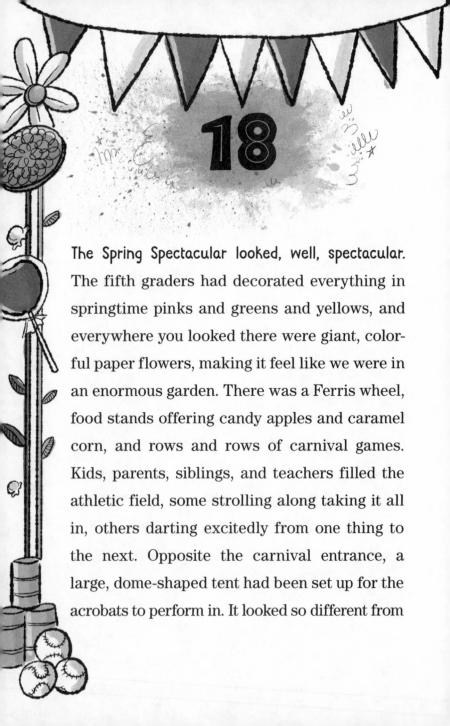

18

The Spring Spectacular looked, well, spectacular. The fifth graders had decorated everything in springtime pinks and greens and yellows, and everywhere you looked there were giant, colorful paper flowers, making it feel like we were in an enormous garden. There was a Ferris wheel, food stands offering candy apples and caramel corn, and rows and rows of carnival games. Kids, parents, siblings, and teachers filled the athletic field, some strolling along taking it all in, others darting excitedly from one thing to the next. Opposite the carnival entrance, a large, dome-shaped tent had been set up for the acrobats to perform in. It looked so different from our regular school field, it was hard to believe this was the same place where our gym teacher makes us do push-ups, which by the way are the dumbest things in the world because I have never ever seen a grown-up stop what they were doing and say, *I think I'll do a push-up. I'm so glad I learned how to do them in school!* The point is, the carnival looked amazing, but I couldn't enjoy any of it because I was picking up garbage with Mapefrl.

"You get that one, Hazy. It's a half-eaten hot dog." He pointed at the ground.

"Why do *I* have to?" I asked defiantly.

"Because I just picked up the pretzel covered in mud," he said.

I sighed like a grown-up, adjusted my plastic gloves, then picked up the hot dog and threw it in the trash. I wanted to find the kid who dropped it on the ground and say, *See? How hard was that? Pick it up, drop it in the trash!* Sheesh.

I looked around with envy. Everyone else was having so much fun. At the face-painting booth, Lila was carefully painting a rose onto a little girl's cheek. At the petting zoo, Derrick laughed as a miniature goat nibbled out of his hand. At the haunted house, which managed to look pretty spooky even though it was just a pop-up canopy with black plastic hung over it, Milo was wearing his ghost costume, daring people to come inside. And on the very other side of the field, carefully stacking one hundred cupcakes onto a cupcake tower, was Elizabeth.

We hadn't spoken since our fight yesterday. And even though it was only a day, I really missed her. I wondered if she missed me, or if she was just happy I wasn't bugging her about my tomorrow visions. But that wouldn't make sense. She loved my visions. She was fascinated by them (spelling word: *fascinated*, not *them*). She asked me the right questions, helped me organize my thoughts, and even figured out things that I couldn't. She was, well, the perfect side-kick. Now I didn't even know if we were friends anymore.

Mapefrl poked my back with his plastic-covered hand. "Come on. Help me put a new bag in the can over there." We were heading toward a garbage bin that was overflowing with trash when a couple of older kids charged past us. One of them was wearing a plastic hat covered in glitter, which was attractive (the hat, not the kid) yet extremely irritating (the hat, not the kid) because every time he moved, a glob of glit-ter fell off the hat and sprinkled all over the

ground. *Great*, I thought, *more stuff to clean up.* I bent down to scoop it up. And that's when I realized something about the glitter. It was green. And sparkly. My heart pounded in my chest. *Green sparkles.*

I needed to follow those kids.

"Hey, where are you going?" Mapefrl called out, clearly annoyed that I was walking away.

"I see a mess over there!" I called. Well, *fibbed* might be a better word. But I was on a mission to prevent doom. The garbage can would have to wait.

I hurried through the crowd, trying not to lose the glitter-hat kid. He was way ahead of me, but I saw him heading toward the acrobat tent. Lots of other people were gathering there as well. I guess the acrobats were about to per-form.

On my way to the tent, I passed through an archway of colorful balloons and despite my fierce determination to keep track of the glitter-hat kid, I couldn't help but stop and admire how cool it looked. Perhaps I could create something just like it to put in front of my Mars ice-skating rink. Who wouldn't want to enter a rink through something so festive? It was like running through a rainbow of bubbles.

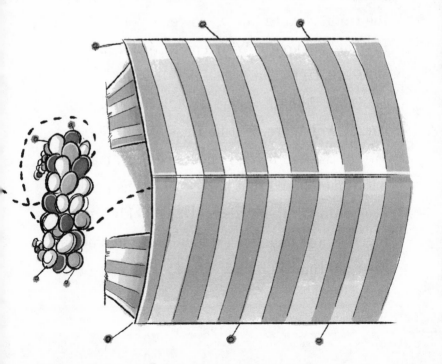

Rainbow bubbles. Another piece of my vision, solved! I believed I was getting closer to the doom.

Inside the tent, the glitter-hat kid kept bobbing in and out of sight, making it hard to keep track of him, especially in such a big crowd. Then it got harder because the lights darkened. Someone whispered for me to sit down, so I grabbed one of the last seats left, in the second row. The glitter-hat kid was just one row over, right in the front. Next to him was a teenager holding a tie-dyed backpack. With a picture of a cat.

Pink, fluffy cat.

Okay, fine, it wasn't exactly a pink fluffy cat. It was more of a hairless, creepy-looking kitten, if we're being honest. But hey, maybe I had remembered that part wrong. The point is, everything from my vision was quickly coming together and I felt like I was in the right place at the right time. For what, I had no idea.

19

Lively music played as eight acrobats tumbled onto the stage. They were wearing the costumes from the poster. Behind them was the backdrop with the lightning bolt. While they were leaping and flipping and twirling through the air, I looked around wildly, trying to spot clues regarding the doom. But I came up short. It wasn't until halfway through the third routine that something made me sit up and take notice.

At that point in the show, one of the acrobats playfully tumbled into the audience and took the green-glitter hat from the kid. The kid I believed had something to do with the doom! He laughed as the acrobat put the hat on her own head, then hopped back onstage. Then the other acrobats started passing the hat to one another in a series of stunts, including one where a performer did a full backflip with the hat staying completely on his head! My first thought was: I could totally do that. My second thought was: now the glitter hat was onstage. And that meant something bad was probably going to happen there.

My eyes darted around. Was something going to tip over? Collapse? Break? Also, would doing that backflip hat trick get me on TV? I needed to focus. I squinted and glanced up at a sparkly disco ball rotating above the stage. Actually, it wasn't rotating as much as kind

of swaying back and forth. I hoped it didn't fall. That would really distract me from preventing doom. Then I remembered the final part of my vision: *falling object*. Anxiously, I looked at the acrobats, then back at the swaying disco ball. And right there and then, I knew what was going to happen. The disco ball was going to fall. I jumped up from my seat and ran for the stage.

As I got closer, I tried to think of all the ways I could get up to the disco ball in time:

1. Ladder (don't have one).
2. Jumping (too short).
3. Flying (can't).
4. Magic (not real).

Onstage, the acrobats were forming a human

pyramid. I checked the disco ball. It was swaying faster now. There was no time to wait. I
climbed onto the stage.

Needless to say, the acrobats were a tad surprised to see a third grader standing there in the
middle of their show. But then, all of a sudden,
one of them lifted me up into the air! Everyone
in the audience gasped. Someone clapped her
hand over her mouth like she could not believe
what she was seeing. And what she was seeing
was me being lifted to the top of the pyramid! I
felt weightless, like I was floating. I felt . . . like
I was in space! Little had I known I would be doing
this kind of preparation for my Mars mission!

Before I knew it, I was at the tippy top of the
pyramid, and I didn't know what to do. So I
started to perform. I stuck my arms in the air.
I lifted one leg up behind me. I started doing
the Funky Chicken. And guess what? Everyone
cheered!

And then I realized I was directly under the swaying disco ball. This was my chance! I stretched my arm, trying to reach it, but instead I batted it away, making it sway even more. Then the worst thing happened, for real live. I slipped, which caused me to scream, which caused the other acrobats to scream, which made the entire pyramid wobble like crazy. And then we all went toppling down.

I should probably leave the performing to Elizabeth.

One of the acrobats helped me up and asked if I was hurt, and when I said no she started shouting at me to get off the stage, which I think was a rather abrupt change in tone after being so worried about me one second before. But then the other acrobats joined in, and soon they were all yelling at me to get off the stage. Then the audience starting booing. Someone started throwing popcorn. It was noisy, it was chaotic, it was completely out of control. The point is, I don't think astronauts have to deal with this kind of thing. Also, I still had to prevent the doom.

"The disco ball," I yelled desperately, pointing. "It's going to fall."

An acrobat looked up, then shook her finger at me. "That? It's not going to fall. It's supposed to do that!"

My stomach lurched. I had been wrong. About everything. The other performers glared at me, clearly annoyed that I had caused all of this for nothing. My head started throbbing and I felt kind of nauseated. I didn't prevent doom. I created a disaster.

So here's what I did next.

I ran.

20

"Ooooooooo! Oooooooooooooo!" I could hear the fifth graders inside the haunted house trying to make spooky ghost noises. I could tell which one was Milo by the way he made his voice rise super high and quiver like crazy. It was even more annoying than before, but maybe that's because I'd been hiding behind the haunted house for the past hour. And I was never coming out. After falling onstage, ruining the acrobat show, completely humiliating myself, and worst of all, doing it all for nothing because I was totally wrong about my vision, I had decided to stay here, away from everyone on the planet, for the rest of my life.

Except I kind of wanted a candy apple.

As I wrestled with the difficult choice of never moving again or taking just a few minutes to get a yummy snack, I was interrupted by a voice next to me. It was Elizabeth.

"Hi, Hazy Bloom," she said quietly. Honestly? I didn't know Elizabeth could speak quietly. But it wouldn't have mattered if she was screeching like a baboon (which come to think of it was what Milo sounded like in the haunted house). I was just so happy to see her.

"Hi," I said back.

"I heard what happened at the show," she said. "Are you okay?"

"Yeah, I'm okay." Then I paused. "No, I'm not okay! For real live! Elizabeth, I'm sorry I yelled at you yesterday."

Elizabeth leaned in intensely. "No, *I'm* sorry! I was a pain! I was just worried the cupcakes wouldn't get done—"

"Because of me! I didn't help at all! I was the pain!"

"Well, that's true." She paused. Then she went on. "But you've had a lot on your mind. And it all worked out anyway because May helped me and . . . well . . . I just really miss you. And I want us to be friends again."

"Me, too! I want that, too!" I said. "And I totally want you to be my sidekick. Okay?"

"Okay." Elizabeth smiled. Boy, did I feel better! It was so nice to have my best friend back. We sat leaning against the haunted house for a minute. And that's when I remembered why I was hiding there. I covered my face with my hands.

"Oh, Elizabeth, it was awful." I told her about the green-glitter hat, and the rainbow balloons, and the swinging disco ball, and how I was wrong about all of it.

Elizabeth chewed on her lip for a minute. Then she said, "Okay, let's just think about this. We can figure it out." And I totally believed her.

But then May appeared and told Elizabeth the judging for the cupcake contest was starting.

On the field, the long table was being wheeled over with all the cupcake displays on it, and right at the end was Elizabeth's cupcake tower. Even from here I could see that it looked amazing.

"Wow!" I said. "Your cupcake tower looks *incredibleous*" (not a spelling word, or any word, but totally should be).

"Thanks." Elizabeth smiled

proudly. And that's when I saw that each of her one hundred cupcakes was in a sparkly, green-glitter wrapper.

Elizabeth and I looked at each other, realizing the same thing at the same time. We jumped up and started running as fast as our superhero and sidekick legs would carry us.

Music pumped through the carnival speakers, making it feel like we were in a superhero movie. Maybe that's why when I saw Mapefrl in my way I yelled, "Move, kid, I'm saving the day!" It just felt like the right thing to say. Even though he ignored me and then I tripped over his foot.

Up ahead was another balloon archway, just like the first one, and we ran through it. Maybe that was the one I was supposed to pay attention to. I still really liked it.

We got to the contest just as the judging began. May was in the front, waving for Elizabeth to come over. But there was already a crowd gathered, and we couldn't get closer. We were trapped in the back. At the cupcake table were the judges, who were actually just teachers. Mrs. Agnes was one of them. They were walking around the table, carefully observing each display and marking their clipboards importantly like they were analyzing a new species of jellyfish, not looking at homemade cupcakes at a school carnival. I noticed that the table wobbled like crazy whenever somebody touched it. It looked about a thousand years old. I might suggest the school use some of the money from the carnival to buy new furniture.

Across the crowd, I saw Kingston (remember him, the fifth-grade version of Mapefrl?) running around. It didn't seem like he cared at all about the contest because he wasn't even paying attention; instead, he was being annoying and waving around the biggest, fluffiest stick of pink cotton candy I'd ever seen. Like, extra-fluffy, for real live.

Fluffy, pink . . .

The fluffy pink cat from my vision came rushing back. Only now I realized it wasn't a cat at all. It was cotton candy. Wild!

Now I had figured out everything from my vision, except for one thing: the falling object.

Kingston and his cotton candy were getting closer to the cupcake table. The judges didn't notice and continued their judging. One of them brushed against the table and it wobbled even more.

Suddenly, I knew what the falling object was. It was Elizabeth's cupcake tower.

"Catch the cupcakes, catch the cupcakes!" I hollered. But we were too far away and the music was blaring, so no one could hear me. I tried to push through the crowd, but there were too many people in the way. How was I going to get through? How would I save the cupcakes? Then I got an idea.

"CaaaaaaaaYAAAYAYAYAYAYAAAA!" I shrieked. It was the loudest, best birdcall I had done yet. Aunt Jenna would have been impressed. Everyone stared at me, probably wondering why I was calling birds in the middle of the carnival. Also, it's possible they thought I was crazy because as I charged forward, they jumped right out of my way. So my plan worked. I ran straight to the end of the table. Mrs. Agnes looked at me in surprise.

"Hazel, what are you *doing*?" she whispered harshly.

"Saving the cupcakes!" I whispered back.

Mrs. Agnes looked around. "What are you talking about? Nothing is happening to the cupcakes!"

"It will," I declared. And then it did. At that very moment, Kingston, still not paying attention, tripped over a leg of the thousand-year-old table. The leg buckled, the entire table tipped downward, and all the cupcake displays began sliding toward the ground, the first one being Elizabeth's. And I was right there to catch it.

I. Saved. Elizabeth's. Cupcakes. From. Doom. Which in my opinion was kind of better than making them.

Elizabeth swooped in and grabbed the other side of the display because let me tell you, holding a tower of one hundred cupcakes all by yourself is no walk in the park. We carefully set it down on a nearby picnic table while the teachers grabbed the rest of the displays and set them down, too. Elizabeth and I quickly checked that all the cupcakes were okay, which they were. Then we started jumping up and down and hugging and laughing and *woohoo*ing. Wow, we were good!

Mrs. Agnes turned to us, grinning from ear to ear. "Girls, that was amazing!" Then her expression switched from happy to baffled. "But Hazel. How on earth did you know that was going to happen?"

"Oh, just a hunch," I said. Elizabeth and I

smiled at each other and squeezed hands. Off to the side, I saw a teacher escorting Kingston and his cotton candy to his parents, who did not seem pleased. That made me smile even more.

Then, to ruin the moment as usual, the original Mapefrl bulldozed over. I was sure he was about to yell at me about picking up garbage, but instead he said, "Hey, good job, Hazy Bloom." And he kind of smiled.

Maybe he wasn't the most annoying person ever.

Then he burped in my face.

Okay, he still was.

21

The rest of the carnival was a blast, and I say this even though I went right back to picking up trash. The truth is, after all the craziness I had just been through with my tomorrow vision, the acrobat show, and the cupcake-saving, I wanted to do something boring and simple that had nothing to do with tomorrow power. Trash pickup was just the thing.

I even told Mapefrl to go take a break and I'd do it on my own for a while. That's how happy I was about how everything had turned out: I did a nice thing for Mapefrl. He gave me a sort of goofy smile, then headed straight to the "messy zone," where you got to play with icky things like Silly String, shaving cream, cooked spaghetti, and lots of other stuff. The Baby would have loved it. Speaking of the The Baby, toward the end of the carnival, Mom, Dad, The Baby, and Aunt Jenna all showed up to check it out. I recommended the haunted house to them. And reminded them to throw away their trash.

Did I mention Elizabeth won the cupcake contest? Well, she did! At the end of the carnival, they called her name in front of everyone and handed her a big gift certificate for Camp Showbiz. She gave a short speech where she thanked May for helping her at the last minute, her mom for buying the ingredients, and me for saving her cupcakes from doom. Everyone laughed at that, but only we knew why it was so funny.

After her speech, Elizabeth ran up to me. "Camp Showbiz, here I come!" she said, making jazz hands. I think she's a natural, for real live.

Me? I'll stick to space travel. Except I am pretty great at the Funky Chicken.

That evening, my family took Aunt Jenna out to dinner for her last night in town. At the restaurant, the two of us cracked everyone up with our birdcalls. Even Milo attempted one or two.

To my relief, I didn't have any visions for the rest of the day—well, except for one where I saw the shape of a star, but I honestly didn't give it much thought. After all the excitement of the carnival, I figured I could ignore a vision for once. Although I was kind of curious what it meant.

· · · · ·

By Sunday afternoon, I was feeling tired and content. Everything seemed to have worked out just how it was supposed to. And I really got to

166

like having Aunt Jenna around. So when I saw her wheeling her suitcase out of my room I was more than a little bummed. "Are you going now?" I asked her, even though I knew the answer.

"Afraid so," she said, smiling.

Aunt Jenna crouched down next to me. "I'll visit again soon. Promise," she said, hugging me tightly. "'Bye, Hazy Bloom," she whispered. "I had a lot of fun with you this week. I think you and I need to do a better job of staying in touch.

Who knows, we might have lots to talk about." Then with a little wave she headed toward the door, where Dad was waiting to drive her to the airport.

"Oh, I almost forgot!" She reached into her purse and pulled out a small polka-dot box. "For you," she said. Then she left.

I opened the box and found a pretty silver chain—a necklace, with one single charm hanging at the bottom. A star.

All of a sudden, I got the weirdest tingly feeling in the whole world, not because I was having a tomorrow vision, but because I was beginning to realize something. I started thinking hard about all the kooky things from this past week with Aunt Jenna and how they actually weren't so kooky after all. The rain boots just before a rare rainy day, the advance notice of the word *jubilant*, the birdcalls that  saved the cup- cakes. In fact, I thought, my pulse quickening, almost every gift or idea from Aunt Jenna turned out to be something I needed . . . the very next day.

Could it be . . . Was it possible . . . ?

Did Aunt Jenna have tomorrow power?

As Dad pulled out of the driveway, Aunt Jenna waved to me through the car window. And as she did, I thought I saw her give me the slightest, tiniest little nod. A nod that said I was right.

Dazed, I went back into the living room, where The Baby was hiccupping in between saying "Beefrechenutz," and his newest word, "Spelft," while Milo was trying to juggle grapes, all of which dropped onto the floor and were immediately eaten by Mr. Cheese. It was back to chaos as usual. But today I didn't mind one bit. Because I was pretty sure I had just discovered something incredible.

I plopped down on the couch, thinking about the past two weeks with this new crazy power of mine. Yes, it got annoying and in some cases almost ruined things completely, like an entire acrobatic performance, my friendship with Elizabeth, and my feelings toward cupcakes.

But it also ended up being pretty great. More than great. In fact, it might be the best thing that's ever happened to me. The Baby wobbled up to me and planted a kiss on my knee and I tickled him back. I wondered what new wild adventures my power would bring. I guess I would just have to wait and see what happened tomorrow. For real live.

GOFISH

JENNIFER HAMBURG

What did you want to be when you grew up?
A Broadway performer. I would put on large-scale productions in my house and make everyone in my family come and watch. I had costumes, props, tickets, the works. I don't know how good the shows were, but I sure had fun doing them.

When did you realize you wanted to be a writer?
As a kid, I was always writing stories and plays, and I even wrote a chapter book in second grade with my friend. But it wasn't until I was an adult that I started thinking, "Hey, maybe this writing thing can be like . . . my JOB."

What's your most embarrassing childhood memory?
I once got the hiccups during a class presentation and couldn't stop. Very bad timing.

What's your favorite childhood memory?
Dancing in *The Nutcracker*. I was one of Mother Ginger's children.

As a young person, who did you look up to most?
My third-grade teacher. She introduced me to more books than I can remember, and she made every classroom

activity just so creative and fun. Also, for some reason, she had us learn all fifty states and their capitals, including spellings and abbreviations. We had to take a test every week until we got it right. It was a pain at the time, but I can promise you, to this day I know every single U.S. capital—you can quiz me!

What was your favorite thing about school?
I loved reading and writing (of course!), but we also had a really amazing music and dance program, which I adored. In high school, for reasons I never figured out, I was also outstanding in chemistry.

What were your hobbies as a kid? What are your hobbies now?
I loved to play outside with friends, ride my bike, put on plays (see first question!), jump on my pogo stick (I won a neighborhood record for pogo stick jumping), and read. These days, I like to explore new places with my kids, do crossword puzzles, take my dog to the dog park, and read (some things never change).

Did you play sports as a kid?
The closest I came to sports was gymnastics. If bowling and roller-skating count, add those to the list!

What was your first job, and what was your "worst" job?
My first job was at Marble Slab Creamery as an ice cream server. It was also my best job because we got to take home leftover ice cream every day. My worst job was as a waitress at a breakfast-only restaurant. I had to wake up

while it was still dark and be there by 4:45 am. And I'm not a morning person. That job didn't last long.

What book is on your nightstand now?
On my actual nightstand is a stack of book-bound screenplays that I'm working my way through. On my virtual nightstand—my iPhone—I'm reading a book called *When You Reach Me* by Rebecca Stead.

How did you celebrate publishing your first book?
I'm not sure I did, because I was a new parent at the time and exhausted, so I'm pretty sure I just went to bed. But I've gotten much better at celebrating since then.

Where do you write your books?
I have a beautiful desk with a comfy chair near a bright and sunny window . . . but I write on my living room couch.

What sparked your imagination for *Hazy Bloom?*
I wanted to write a story about a funny, quirky, smart, relatable girl—someone who kids felt like they knew. I remember that age so well, the way you could feel goofy and excited and worried and frustrated all at the same time. I spent a lot of time getting to know Hazy as a character, and only after that did I ask myself, "What would be the craziest thing that could happen to this kid?" And "tomorrow power" was the answer!

What challenges do you face in the writing process, and how do you overcome them?
The first steps are the hardest, when I'm working out the big plot points and how the story and subplots will play out.

Figuring out Hazy's visions, for example, was a big challenge. I remember making a chart that listed each vision, then I broke it down into: what she sees, what she *thinks* it means, and what it *actually* means. It takes a lot of planning—and patience—but it's always worthwhile!

What is your favorite word?
Haberdashery.

If you could live in any fictional world, what would it be?
Oz.

Who is your favorite fictional character?
Willy Wonka. Also, I'm super fond of Mo Willems' Pigeon.

What was your favorite book when you were a kid? Do you have a favorite book now?
As a kid, I read every Judy Blume book about fifty times, but I don't think I could pick a favorite (okay, if you forced me: *Otherwise Known as Sheila the Great*). I also loved Roald Dahl and Shel Silverstein. I have most of the poems from *Where the Sidewalk Ends* memorized.

If you could travel in time, where would you go and what would you do?
I'd travel to the future to see if we ever did get cars to fly.

What's the best advice you have ever received about writing?
I once read this and it stuck: *It's never as bad as you think, and it's never as good as you think.* I have no idea why that's comforting, but it is.

What advice do you wish someone had given you when you were younger?
That it's okay to change your mind again and again and again.

Do you ever get writer's block? What do you do to get back on track?
Writer's block is very real! Oftentimes, however, I get the opposite of writer's block—where I have so many competing ideas, I end up all over the place. When either of these things happen (which are both fine and part of the process!), I usually break things down into tiny pieces: first, figure out *one thing* about this chapter. Now, the next thing, and the next. This makes it much more doable. If that fails, I leave the house and get some frozen yogurt. That always works, too.

What do you want readers to remember about your books?
I'd hope that kids remember Hazy like she was a friend, because that would mean she really connected with them as a character. I also hope they remember that they laughed so hard, milk came out of their nose. It's a big hope, but still.

What would you do if you ever stopped writing?
Sometime during the beginning of my career, I received two job offers: to write for a new preschool TV series, or to be a career counselor for college students. I almost took the counseling job, so I suppose that's what I would do . . . although I'm glad I took the other path for now!

If you were a superhero, what would your superpower be?
The power to say something once and have my kids actually respond.

Do you have any strange or funny habits? Did you when you were a kid?
I still have my baby blanket. And NO, I don't sleep with it! But I do keep it close by.

What do you consider to be your greatest accomplishment?
My kids. And that I finally started making my bed every day.

What would your readers be most surprised to learn about you?
I worked on the show *Sesame Street* and was once in charge of driving Big Bird to lunch.

It's the annual Third Grade Leadership Challenge, where each third-grade class plans and hosts a fundraiser. If Hazy shows responsibility by leading her class to victory, will her parents get her the pet of her dreams? (Spoiler alert: it's not a kitten or a puppy.)

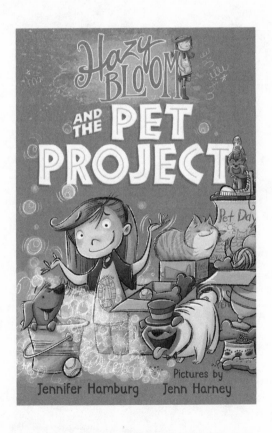

KEEP READING FOR AN EXCERPT.

My name is Hazy Bloom, and I can see tomorrow. Not next year, not two weeks from now, tomorrow. Here's how it works: I will be enjoying my day, doing something totally normal, like counting toilet-paper squares, or searching for alien life, or trying to make my own toothpaste, when all of a sudden a "tomorrow vision" will flash into my head of something that's going to happen the next day. Sometimes the vision is crystal clear, and other times it's, well, hazy (ha!). Either way, it's up to me to figure out what the vision means. The good news is, I always get it right.

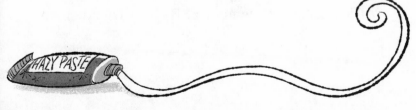

Well, except for the time I turned around all the desks in my classroom as a prank because I was sure we were having a substitute (we weren't). And that other time I snuck out of science lab because I was positive a wagon full of raw eggs was about to plow into a ticket booth (it didn't). Then there was the whole Spring Spectacular catastrophe, where I ruined an acrobatic show in front of the entire school . . .

Okay, fine. I'm not always right. See, my tomorrow power is pretty new. I'm still trying to figure out how it works, how I got it in the first place, and whether I'll be getting any other powers soon, such as dolphin translation or invisibility, which would come in very handy in gym class when we are forced to do push-ups. The point is, I'm getting a new iguana.

Let me back up a bit. It all started this morning, when Elizabeth and I arrived at the school office. Elizabeth is my BFSB (best friend since birth) and my official "tomorrow power side-kick," which is a job she gave herself but I completely agreed to. Whenever I get a tomorrow vision, Elizabeth is the first to know (besides me, of course). Then she helps me figure out if the vision is about something good (sometimes), bad (most of the time), or wonderful (pretty much never). The point is, if you ever end up with a superpower and need a side-kick, well, you can't call Elizabeth. Because she works with me. Also, I just like having her around because, as my best friend, she's funny, smart, and basically the nicest person in the whole world.

HAZY BLOOM, get over here right now!

She's also a teensy bit bossy.

See, Elizabeth gets a little intense when we have something important to do. And this morning, the two of us had been picked to do the morning announcements at school. As far as Elizabeth was concerned, that was right up there with becoming president or discovering a new planet or holding the door open on the way to recess. In other words, very important.

"Girls, this is *so* exciting!" That was our teacher, Mrs. Agnes. She obviously thought this was important, too, the way she was darting back and forth like we were about to go on national television instead of our school video monitor. "Are you ready? Are you nervous? Do you have everything?"

Elizabeth waved two pieces of paper in her hand. "Everything's right here!" Mrs. Agnes didn't have to worry. Elizabeth was ready. She handed me my paper, which looked like a movie script. It had carefully highlighted lines, some with *ELIZABETH* in front and others with *HAZEL* (my real name) in front. I couldn't help but notice that there were a lot more *ELIZABETH*s than *HAZEL*s. But that was fine with me. She's the performer. I'm the secret superhero.

"Okay, this is it! Places, please!" Mrs. Agnes squealed.

Elizabeth smoothed her shirt and checked that we were standing behind the white line marked on the floor (she was; I was not). Then she nodded professionally to Mrs. Agnes, who pushed a button on the side of the camera. It started blinking.

"It's on!" Mrs. Agnes cried for the whole school to hear as an image of Elizabeth and me flashed onto the video monitors in every classroom. Elizabeth was smiling pleasantly into the camera. She looked happy, comfortable, and confident.

I looked like I was trying to remember when I had last gone to the bathroom.

Mrs. Agnes pointed at us and mouthed, "Action!"

"Good morning and happy Friday, Lipkin Lions!" Elizabeth announced.

In case you're wondering what in the world that means: our school is called Ida Lipkin Elementary School, and our school mascot is the lion. I don't know why it's a lion, because if you

ask me, it should be something much more ex-
otic, like the Lipkin Llamas or the Lipkin Lemurs
or the Lipkin Squids (who says it has to begin
with an *L*?). The point is, I was busy thinking
up different animal mascots and totally missed
my turn to speak.

"Hazy Bloom, go!" Elizabeth hissed. She
jabbed her finger at my paper.

"Oh!" I said, fumbling for my line. I began.
"My name is Hazy Bloom. And—"

"And here are today's announcements!"
Elizabeth interrupted.

I guess she wanted to say that part.

Elizabeth went on to announce the science-
fair finalists. Then she talked about the school
clothing drive, which was still accepting dona-
tions. Then she reminded everyone to order their
yearbooks before the deadline next Friday. Then
she performed the song "You're a Grand Old
Flag," which I don't think was planned, but it

did seem like an effective way for Elizabeth to broadcast her talents to the whole school.

After Elizabeth finished the song, she gestured that it was my turn to speak again. I looked down at my paper.

"And now, the thought of the day." All I had to do was read the quote written on my paper and I'd be finished. Simple. Easy. Done and done.

Except at that very moment, just as I was about to speak . . . a tomorrow vision flashed into my head.

That's how it happens. I'll be doing something perfectly normal, like reading the thought of the day in front of the whole school, when suddenly, I start to feel prickles and goose bumps and my body gets hot and cold at the same time, and then—a picture flashes in my head.

And this picture was of . . . a bright yellow blob.